My J Book

by Jane Belk Moncure

illustrated by Linda Hohag

THE CHILD'S WORLD

ELGIN, ILLINOIS 60120

Library of Congress Cataloging in Publication Data

Moncure, Jane Belk.
  My "i" book.

  (My first steps to reading)
  Rev. ed. of: My i sound box. © 1979.
  Summary: Little i fills his box with many things
beginning with the letter "i."
  1. Children's stories, American.   [1. Alphabet]
I. Hohag, Linda. ill.   II. Moncure, Jane Belk.   My i
sound box.   III. Title.   IV. Series: Moncure, Jane
Belk.   My first steps to reading.
PZ7.M739Myi   1984   [E]   84-17543
ISBN 0-89565-283-8

Distributed by Childrens Press, 1224 West Van Buren Street,
Chicago, Illinois 60607.

My "j" Book

Little  j had a box.

It was a yellow box.

He said, "I will fill my  box."

But first Little j put on
his jeans and jacket.

7

Then he  jumped over

his box like a jumping jack.

Then he
jumped into
his box.

"I am a jack-
in-the-box!"
he said.

He jumped up a hill,

jump,

jump,

jump ...

He jumped down a hill,

jump,

jump,

jump.

Then he found a ...

jack-o'-lantern.

Guess where he
put it?

box

Then he jumped some more.

Jump!

Jump!

He found jack rabbits,
jumping jack rabbits.

"In you go, jack rabbits,"
he said.

Then Little J found jays.
"Jay, jay, jay," they said.

Little  put the jays into his box.

Little  found a jeep.

He jumped into the jeep.

18

He drove into the  jungle.

He found a jaguar.

The jaguar was about to jump on the jack rabbits!

Little **J** held the jack-o'-lantern up,

and the  jaguar

jumped away.

Little  caught the jaguar.

jail

He put it
in jail so it
could not jump on
the jack rabbits.

Little  saw

Jumbo, the jolly elephant.

Jumbo was too big for the box.

Little  found a jet, a jumbo jet,

Jumbo   jack rabbits

jumbo jet

for all his things.

jack-o'-lantern   jay   jacket and jeans

jays

More words with Little .

jar

jonquil

jacks

jade

jellyfish

jackal

jewelry

January

s	m	t	w	t	f	s
1	2	3	4	5	6	7
8	9	10	11	12	13	14
15	16	17	18	19	20	21
22	23	24	25	26	27	28
29	30	31				

June

s	m	t	w	t	f	s
				1	2	3
4	5	6	7	8	9	10
11	12	13	14	15	16	17
18	19	20	21	22	23	24
25	26	27	28	29	30	

July

s	m	t	w	t	f	s
						1
2	3	4	5	6	7	8
9	10	11	12	13	14	15
16	17	18	19	20	21	22
23/30	24/31	25	26	27	28	29

juggler

jelly

juice

29